This Little Tiger
book belongs to:

_____

_____

_____

To Linda and John, for being
such nice neighbours
~ CF

For Mick, with love
~ GH

LITTLE TIGER PRESS
An imprint of Magi Publications
1 The Coda Centre, 189 Munster Road, London SW6 6AW
www.littletigerpress.com

First published in Great Britain 2004
This edition published 2005

Text copyright © Claire Freedman 2004
Illustrations copyright © Gaby Hansen 2004
Claire Freedman and Gaby Hansen have asserted their rights to
be identified as the author and illustrator of this work under the
Copyright, Designs and Patents Act, 1988

A CIP catalogue record for this book is available from the British Library

Printed in Singapore by Tien Wah Press Pte. Ltd.

2 4 6 8 10 9 7 5 3 1

Oops-a-Daisy!

Claire Freedman

illustrated by

Gaby Hansen

LITTLE TIGER PRESS

LONDON

There was a lot of jumping and thumping
over in the meadow. Mama Rabbit was
teaching Daisy how to hop.
 "I'm going to try hopping all by
myself!" Daisy cried excitedly.
"Watch me, Mama!"

Daisy took a huge leap,
lost her balance and fell
over backwards!

"Never mind!" said
Mama Rabbit. "Try again."
Daisy did!

Trippity-uppity
OOPS!

Hippity-hoppity
FLOP!

"I don't think I can do it, Mama!" Daisy cried.

"No one gets it right first time," Mama Rabbit said, picking Daisy up and dusting her down. "Look at Little Mouse over by the duck pond!"

Mama Mouse was showing Little Mouse
how to climb the reeds to reach
the golden seedheads.

Little Mouse inched closer
and closer. She had almost
reached the top when . . .

. . . slippity-zippity! She slid
down again with a bump!
"Learning new things can be
hard for everyone!" Daisy said.

Daisy decided to practise little bunny hops.
  "Keep in a straight line," Mama Rabbit
called. "That's it!"
  Up down, up down wobbled Daisy
through the tall grass.
  "Hooray, I can do it!" she
cried. "Small hops
are easier!"

Daisy saw a
big molehill ahead.
She jumped a huge jump.

Whoopsity-oopsity!

"Ouch! Who put that prickly
thistle there?" Daisy said.
"And why won't my feet
do what I tell them to?"

"They will, in time," said
Mama Rabbit. She helped Daisy
up and gave her a cuddle. "Have
you seen the mess Little Badger
is making?"

Little Badger was out in
the field, learning how to
dig tunnels.

Crashity-smashity!

Suddenly another one of his tunnels collapsed. Little Badger and Daddy Badger were getting muddier and muddier!

"I'm glad I'm not the only one who needs more practise," giggled Daisy.

Daisy and Mama Rabbit rested by the duck
pond. Blue-green dragonflies darted
around them whizzily-busily.

"Gribbit!" A big frog hopped out
through the bulrushes.

"I wish I could jump like that!"
said Daisy. "Do you think I ever will?"

"You'll jump even higher!" her
mama replied.

"Really?" cried Daisy, leaping up.
"I'll have another go!"

"One, two . . . one, two,"
counted Daisy as she bounced.
"Whee, look at me! Hopping
is fun!"

"That's much better," Mama
Rabbit called. "Oh, watch out,
Daisy!" . . .

Bumpity-thumpity!

Daisy slithered down the slippery
bank and skidded into the pond!

"Gribbit, gribbit!" croaked the
frog in surprise.

"Help!" Daisy cried. "I'm
stuck in the mud!"

Mama Rabbit ran down and
pulled Daisy free.
  "I was so busy counting that
I didn't see the pond," sighed Daisy.
"There's so much to remember
all at once!"

"Cheer up, Daisy," Mama Rabbit
said. "Let's practise together."
Paw in paw, Daisy and
Mama Rabbit hopped and
skipped round and round the
duck pond.

Little Duckling was out on the water, practising his swimming. "Little Duckling isn't doing very well," said Daisy. "He can only swim in tiny circles!"

Then suddenly . . .

. . . splashity-crashity!

Little Duckling sailed right into some water lilies! Quickly his mama swam across to untangle him.

"There's someone else who didn't look where they were going!" Mama Rabbit smiled.

Daisy laughed. "I'm going to try hopping by myself one more time!" she said.

Up down, up down bounced Daisy.
Wibbly-wobbly, hippity-hoppity hop!
 "That's it!" cried her mama. "Keep going!"
 "Did you see how high I jumped?" called Daisy
proudly. "I was almost flying! I can do it, Mama! I can do it!"
 "Oh well done, Daisy!" said Mama Rabbit, giving her
a big hug. "You're hopping!"

Daisy hopped . . .

and skipped . . .

and hopped.

At last her legs were too
tired to take her any further!
 "I'll have to carry you
home this evening!" her
mama laughed.

Happily Daisy climbed into Mama Rabbit's
arms and buried herself snuggly-huggly
into her soft warm fur.
  "Do you think Little Mouse, Little Badger
and Little Duckling learnt how to climb
and dig and swim?" she asked her
mama sleepily.

"Oh, I'm sure they did!"
Mama Rabbit whispered.
"In the end!"

Books to inspire you! – from Little Tiger Press

You're Too Small!
Shen Roddie
Steve Lavis

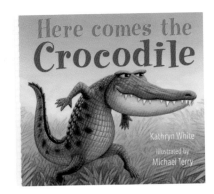

Here comes the Crocodile
Kathryn White
illustrated by
Michael Terry

LITTLE BEAR'S SPECIAL WISH
GILLIAN LOBEL
illustrated by
GABY HANSEN

Goose on the Loose
Claire Freedman
Illustrated by
Vanessa Cabban

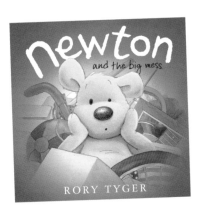

newton
and the big mess
RORY TYGER

For information regarding
any of the above titles or for
our catalogue, please contact us:
Little Tiger Press, 1 The Coda Centre,
189 Munster Road, London SW6 6AW
Tel: 020 7385 6333 • Fax: 020 7385 7333
E-mail: info@littletiger.co.uk
www.littletigerpress.com